Pee Wee
Pool Party

OTHER BOOKS YOU WILL ENJOY:

GEORGE WASHINGTON CARVER, *Sam and Beryl Epstein*
A GIFT FOR TÍA ROSA, *Karen T. Taha*
A GRAIN OF RICE, *Helena Clare Pittman*
MOLLY'S PILGRIM, *Barbara Cohen*
MAKE A WISH, MOLLY, *Barbara Cohen*
COUNT YOUR MONEY WITH THE POLK STREET SCHOOL,
Patricia Reilly Giff
THE POSTCARD PEST, *Patricia Reilly Giff*
LOOK OUT, WASHINGTON, D.C.!, *Patricia Reilly Giff*

YEARLING BOOKS are designed especially to entertain and enlighten young people. Patricia Reilly Giff, consultant to this series, received her bachelor's degree from Marymount College and a master's degree in history from St. John's University. She holds a Professional Diploma in Reading and a Doctorate of Humane Letters from Hofstra University. She was a teacher and reading consultant for many years, and is the author of numerous books for young readers.

Pee Wee
Pool Party

JUDY DELTON

Illustrated by Alan Tiegreen

A YEARLING BOOK

Published by
Bantam Doubleday Dell Books for Young Readers
a division of
Bantam Doubleday Dell Publishing Group, Inc.
1540 Broadway
New York, New York 10036

ISBN: 0-440-40980-2

Printed in the United States of America

September 1996

10 9 8 7 6 5 4 3

CWO

For Patty Lou Slater Pyne,
who shares with me long-ago memories of
Courtesy Counts, St. Clair streetCars, Cousin
Weak Eyes, Canasta, Car beds, ancient dead Cats,
and a Covey of other Covert anomalies

Contents

CHAPTER 1

Pool Plans for Jody

"**N**o more pencils, no more books!" cried Roger White. "No more teachers' dirty looks!"

Running across the school playground, Roger crumpled up his math folder and his report card and threw them over his head.

"He's littering," said Mary Beth Kelly to her best friend, Molly Duff.

"And he can't throw away a report card!" said Molly.

"I just did!" shouted Roger. "School's out at last. I can throw away anything I want."

It was June. Summer had arrived and so had vacation time. The Pee Wees were looking forward to summer vacation. Roger most of all.

The other Pee Wees liked school. And they liked their Pee Wee meetings, and earning badges. They met all year long at the home of their leader, Mrs. Peters. There was no vacation from being a Pee Wee, and Molly was glad. She loved being a Pee Wee.

"My mom says Roger is going to grow up to be an airhead," said Tracy Barnes.

"He is one already," said Rachel Myers. "He gets bad marks because he never pays attention in school and he never does his homework."

Roger was making faces at the girls now,

and taking off his sneakers to walk barefoot. "I'm going fishing with my dad every single day," he boasted.

"He can't go fishing every day," corrected Patty Baker. "His dad has to go to work some days."

"We're going to California with Ashley for two weeks," said Kenny Baker, Patty's twin brother. Ashley was their cousin and a temporary Pee Wee when she was in town. In California she belonged to the Saddle Scouts.

"We're going to Disneyland while we're there," added Patty.

"We went to Disneyland last year," said Jody George. Jody was in a wheelchair. Molly thought it would be hard to go to Disneyland in a wheelchair, and go on rides and in castles and on boats. But nothing seemed to stop Jody. He did everything the other Pee Wees did.

The Pee Wees stopped in the park and sat down on the benches in the sun.

"Summer feels good on your hair," said Lisa Ronning, leaning back and closing her eyes.

"Guess what?" said Jody. "We're getting a big swimming pool put in our backyard."

"We have one of those," said Rachel. "It has a little ladder and everything. In winter we take it apart and store it."

"Ours is in the ground," said Jody. "It's going to have a diving board."

Jody never liked to hurt anyone's feelings, so he turned to Rachel and added, "But it's probably just like yours, otherwise."

"No it isn't," said Sonny Stone. "Pools that are down in the ground are a lot better. They're just like pools on TV."

"There's nothing the matter with our pool," said Rachel, crossing her arms.

"Ho," said Roger, "yours is just like a big

wading pool compared to the real ones like Jody's getting."

Rachel was turning red. She didn't like to be second best.

The Pee Wees all stared at Jody. Lots of them had wading pools. And there was a lake in town. And a public swimming pool. But no one had a real in-the-ground pool in the backyard!

"What will you do with all the dirt you dig up?" asked Tim Noon.

"They take it away, I guess," said Jody.

"Everybody's got pools in California," said Ashley.

"Well, not many people here do," said Rachel.

"Can we swim in your pool?" asked Kevin Moe. Kevin and Jody were two of Molly's favorite Pee Wees. She had wanted to marry Kevin. Then Jody had joined their troop. She liked him too. Since she couldn't

marry both of them, she decided to wait till she grew up to see what would happen.

"Sure," said Jody. "All my friends can come. After all the pipes are in and it's finished, I'm going to have a big pool party."

Jody was very generous. Molly knew he would share his pool with everyone.

"In California we have these big pool parties, with cold drinks and lots of food and stuff," said Ashley.

"We do that too," said Rachel.

A party with all her friends sounded wonderful to Molly. And there was a new badge to earn. Molly couldn't wait! She was glad school was out, and nothing but fun was ahead!

CHAPTER 2

Water Worries

The next Tuesday was the Pee Wees' meeting day, and the weather was so nice that they met in Mrs. Peters's backyard instead of her basement. Most of them had on shorts and T-shirts. They sat at the picnic table and told all the good deeds they had done since the last meeting. Then they played with baby Nick, Mrs. Peters's baby. When Lucky, Mrs. Peters's dog, brought them the Frisbee, they threw it for him. He was the Pee Wees' mascot.

Mrs. Stone came out of the house with chocolate cupcakes. They had red sprinkles on them. Mrs. Stone was Sonny's mother and the assistant troop leader of the Pee Wees.

Mrs. Peters said, "While you're eating your cupcakes, I have some announcements to make. Are you all listening?"

Some of the Pee Wees were listening. Some of them, including Roger, were not. Sometimes announcements were boring, like the ones about planning rummage sales to earn money for trips. Or the ones about keeping a nature journal. That was too much like school, although Molly loved to write and she loved to read too, and to draw pictures. But most of the Pee Wees didn't like their meetings to feel like school.

As the Pee Wees munched their cupcakes, Mrs. Peters made some boring announcements, and Roger made snoring noises.

But when the announcements were over, Mrs. Peters said, "And now we're going to talk about our new badge!"

Roger stopped snoring, and the Pee Wees sat up straight and clapped and cheered. Sonny whistled through his teeth. Badges were definitely the best thing about being a Pee Wee.

"As you all know, it's summer at last," said their leader. "And so we will be earning a summer badge. A badge for something that we only do in the summer. Or at least, most of the time we do, because it's an outside activity."

"A picnic?" shouted Sonny.

"How can you get a badge for a picnic, dummy?" said Roger, giving Sonny a punch. "Hey, then even the ants could get a badge!" Roger began crawling around on the ground like a large ant. He pretended to crawl up Sonny's leg. Sonny gave him a kick.

Mrs. Peters frowned. She didn't like it when the Pee Wees were rowdy.

"It's better than a picnic," she said. "It's a swimming badge!"

Now Rachel's hand was waving. Everyone knew what she was going to say!

"Mrs. Peters, I have a pool of my own. It will be easy for me to get my badge."

"Well, fine, Rachel, that will be very handy for you."

"I already know how to swim," said Rachel. "I took lessons when I was three, and I can do the dog paddle and the breaststroke and I can even do the jellyfish float."

Now other Pee Wees were waving their hands.

"I can swim too," said Roger. "I can swim as good as a lifeguard!"

Molly noticed that Jody did not raise his hand. He did not tell Mrs. Peters about his new pool. Jody was not a show-off. But Mrs.

Peters should know about his new pool! Someone else should tell her!

Just then, Kevin did.

"Jody's getting a new pool," he said. "A real one."

"And we're all invited to swim in it!" said Lisa.

"And he's having a pool party when it's done," said Tracy.

"Wonderful!" said Mrs. Peters. "The timing is very good! It will be just in time for our new badge!"

Everyone began to talk about the new pool. They all pretended they were already in it. Roger held his nose and pretended to dive in, and Sonny made swimming strokes with his arms.

Mrs. Peters held up her hand. "If you can already swim, then the badge will be an easy one to earn. But it will also be a chance for you to learn some new water activity, like diving or speed swimming. Or you can help others learn to swim. You can work at some extra accomplishment, since you're more advanced."

The hands went down. Ashley frowned.

"How come we have to do more than the guys who can't swim?" said Roger. "That's not fair. If we can swim already, we should just get our badge free."

"To get this water badge," said Mrs. Peters firmly, "everyone should learn something new. Swimming is the first and most important skill for water sports and water safety."

Some of the Pee Wees wished they had not told Mrs. Peters they could swim. Now it meant they would have to do something extra.

Mrs. Peters went on to explain that they would read about water activities, learn about water safety, and study pool rules. Then they would go to the public pool on their own to practice. When they were ready, each Pee Wee would swim alone across the pool while Mrs. Peters watched, to qualify for his or her badge. And some would dive and show the new swimming strokes they had learned.

When the meeting ended, everyone was talking at once about what fun it would be. Everyone Molly talked to seemed to know how to swim.

"I'm going to work on the swan dive," said Ashley.

"I'll get in more practice than anyone," said Rachel. "Well, except Jody. Because I can get up in the middle of the night if I want to and swim. I'll be able to do a really graceful dive by the time we get our badges."

Forget about diving, thought Molly.

Molly could not dive.

And she could not float.

Worst of all, she could not swim! Molly was afraid of water. Every time she went to the beach, she got water up her nose, and it didn't feel good. Once, she got water in her ears and couldn't hear. She hated to get her head wet. Sometimes mean kids like Roger pushed other kids underwater.

Molly loved badges. She loved earning them, and she loved wearing them.

But this was a badge she did *not* want to earn. She did not want to put her head underwater. She knew if she tried to float or swim, she would sink. The summer had looked like so much fun. Now suddenly it was a summer she dreaded.

Would she be the only one who didn't have fun at Jody's pool party?

Would she be the only one afraid to get her head wet?

And worst of all, would she be the only one who did not receive a swimming badge?

CHAPTER 3

The Bumblebee Swimsuit

Molly was in no hurry to get home. Her mother would ask what the Pee Wees had done and what new badge they were going to work on. Molly didn't want to talk about it.

But after Mary Beth turned the corner to run an errand, there was no place to go but home. Mary Beth was on the way to the drugstore to get some new noseplugs.

Mrs. Duff was home from work early.

"I heard about the new swimming badge!" she said. "And on my way home I stopped at Carson's and got you a new swimsuit. Wait till you see it! I knew you'd outgrown last year's suit, and besides you need something special for earning a badge!"

Her mother put down the carrots she was peeling and dried her hands. She motioned for Molly to follow her to the living room. There she picked up a bag with summer flowers all over it, and opened it.

"Look!" she said. "Isn't it beautiful?"

Mrs. Duff held up the suit. It had a cluster of tags hanging from it. It looked tiny. And it was bright yellow with bumblebees all over it!

"It will stretch," said her mom. "It's spandex."

Molly stared at the suit. She knew she should be grateful. But she wasn't. Maybe her mother could take it back.

"It was on sale, so we can't return it, but I know it will fit," her mother said. "It was a lucky find. Swimsuits can be very expensive."

Now Molly felt worse. She looked at the suit dangling from her mother's hands. It was very bright. In fact, it was blinding. It was the kind of suit she could never hide in. She could not be at the pool and not be noticed.

If she wore a swimsuit that was pale blue maybe she could be pool color.

Or if it was green she could blend in with the nearby trees and no one would notice her. She had heard about lizards that turned the color of whatever they were near so that no animal would notice them and eat them.

Well, in this suit, Molly would be eaten. She would light up and flash and sparkle. The suit would scream, "Look at me! Here I am in a new suit and I can't swim."

Even worse, fingers would point. Everyone would say, "That bumblebee over there is the only one without a badge."

"Well?" said her mother. "What do you think?"

"It's nice," Molly said, holding back tears.

"Do you want to try it on?" asked Mrs. Duff.

"Not right now," said Molly. She climbed the stairs to her room and shut the door.

Molly threw herself on her bed and wondered what to do. Maybe she should tell her mother about her worries. But what could her mother do about them? Molly didn't want her mother going to Mrs. Peters and saying, "I'm sorry, but Molly will have to skip this badge. She's afraid of water." Molly would be embarrassed to have her mother know, let alone the Pee Wees' leader! Being afraid of water was like being afraid of—soda pop! Water was something she drank every day! Why would she fear it?

Well, because there was so much of it. There was never enough soda pop around to fill a pool!

Molly thought about telling Mary Beth. But then Mary Beth would feel bad. And what could she actually do about it? Nothing. No, Molly didn't want any of the Pee Wees to know. She would have to solve this alone.

At suppertime Mrs. Duff said, "Show Dad your new swimsuit, Molly."

Molly went to get the suit she had begun to hate. She held it up for her dad. He held his hand over his eyes. "It's a bright one!" he said. "We'll sure spot you in the pool, won't we?"

That wasn't what Molly wanted to hear.

She wanted him to say that swimming was silly.

Or better yet, that the Duffs were taking a long summer trip and would not be back in time for Molly to earn the badge!

"Aren't we going on vacation?" asked Molly. "Aren't we going to Grandma's or to the lake?"

"Later in the summer, perhaps," said Mrs. Duff. "If we go to the lake, it will be a good thing to learn to swim first. This is a well-timed badge!"

"I think we should go now!" cried Molly. "Now is the best time to travel."

Her parents looked startled.

"I could do the packing," Molly volunteered.

"A person would almost think you wanted to *miss* getting this badge!" said her father, laughing.

"I'm just anxious to go on a trip," said Molly. "And I'm anxious to see Grandma."

"Well, that's a relief," said her mother. "I

thought for a minute you didn't like your new swimsuit!"

Molly would have to learn to love it. And she'd have to face the fact that sooner or later, for better or worse, she'd have to get wet.

CHAPTER 4

Once Begun, Half Done

The next morning Molly sat down at her little white desk with a pencil and paper. She would make a list of ways to solve her problem. She always felt better when she made a list.

"Plan A," she wrote. "Run away." But where to? Whom did she know who would harbor a criminal? Anyone in town would call her mother. Even anyone out of town would want to call her mother.

Perhaps she could sleep in a park. That sounded dangerous. And scary. And cold and wet. No, plan A was not practical. It sounded like more problems than just one.

"Plan B," she wrote. "Go stay with Kyle." Kyle was her pen pal. She lived far away. But where would Molly get the money for a plane or train ticket? She was too young to drive. Even if she had a car, which she didn't, it would be illegal.

"Plan C, learn to swim," she wrote. She sighed. Easier said than done. If she asked someone to teach her, that person would know she didn't know how! It would be admitting defeat before she started.

She could practice getting her head wet in her own bathtub. Maybe she could even practice swimming in the tub! But she was too big. If she stretched out to paddle, she would hit the sides of the tub.

Then an idea occurred to her. What if she just *pretended* to swim? What if she had something like an invisible inner tube under her? Would that be cheating? Worse yet, would she be found out and disgraced? And how could she hide an inner tube?

She tried to think of what could hold her up in the water. What could keep her head high and dry? She had seen people bungee jump off high places. Maybe she could bungee jump from a plane over a lake and when she touched the water she'd bounce back!

No, too showy. A plane with Molly hanging out of it in her bumblebee suit would attract too much attention. Besides, where would she get a plane?

There had to be another way. Pretending was a definite maybe. All Molly had to do was come up with something to hold her up in the water. Something that no one could see.

She crossed off the first two items. Then

she put "pretending" as Plan B. Molly left "learn to swim" as Plan A because there was just the slightest chance that she could accidentally learn, and that would be the most honest way.

Now Molly's work was cut out for her. "Once begun, half done," she remembered her grandma telling her. Well, Molly definitely had begun. A list was always a good beginning.

That afternoon, Molly and Mary Beth went to the library to look up water rules. Mrs. Nelson, the librarian, gave them the right book. "So you two are going to be water sprites!" she said to them, smiling.

"What's a sprite?" whispered Molly to Mary Beth when they sat at a table.

"I think it's like an elf," Mary Beth replied.

"Elves don't swim," said Molly. "They're Santa's helpers."

"Well, they must swim in their time off,"

said Mary Beth. "After all, they can't work in the summer. They have to do something. If a librarian tells you something, it's got to be true. Just look at all the books our librarian's read."

Looking at all the books was staggering. Mrs. Nelson was reading one right now. She must be very, very smart, thought Molly.

The girls opened the book on water safety. It looked dull. There were no pictures. And no mention of water sprites *or* elves.

"Never go near water without a safety vest on," they wrote, taking notes.

"What if I want to take a bath?" asked Mary Beth with a chuckle.

"What if I want a drink of water?" asked Molly, laughing.

They both laughed at the picture in their minds of them wearing a big orange life vest every time they went near a sink or bathtub or water fountain!

31

Mrs. Nelson frowned at them and put her fingers to her lips.

The girls stopped talking and laughing.

"Don't stand up in a boat," they wrote next. Then, "Don't swim unless a lifeguard is present."

Mrs. Nelson came over to their table. She handed the girls two more books. In one, Molly saw pictures of a little girl learning to swim. She studied them.

"Water is nothing to fear," she read, "because the human body will float on its own and rise to the surface."

If this was true, thought Molly, then why did people drown? She read on. The book told just what to do to float on your back. Floating on her back appealed to Molly. Then she would not have to put her face in the water! Molly wrote a few things down in her notebook that she wanted to remember.

Before long, some of the other Pee Wees

came into the library to look up water rules. Rachel came over to their table and sat down.

"I know the rules," she said. "But I better write them down in case Mrs. Peters wants to see them."

She sighed. "Even though I can swim and dive and float, I'll still have to do all this stuff, I suppose, to get my badge. It's really boring, though."

"I don't think it's boring," said Mary Beth. "I like it."

Molly didn't think it was boring either. But she didn't like it. She didn't like it one little bit!

CHAPTER 5

On the Bench

Mrs. Nelson frowned at the girls again. Libraries were not places to talk or whisper. The girls finished their work and put their books away. On the way home, Mary Beth and Rachel talked about how easy it was to swim. Molly felt left out. They talked about Jody's new pool and Rachel's pool and pool parties and how to do the swan dive.

"Diving is sooo cool!" said Rachel. "You feel so great sailing through the air like a bird!"

If Molly sailed through the air, she'd fall like a rock.

"I can't wait for our next meeting," said Mary Beth. "We get to go to the pool and practice."

Molly could wait. It was the first time she wasn't anxious to go to a Pee Wee meeting.

But the meeting day came, and Mrs. Peters wrote the water rules on the blackboard.

"We didn't have to go to the library and look them up after all," grumbled Mary Beth.

Their leader showed them water wings and safety vests. She told them always to stay out of deep water. Molly thought maybe they were not going to the pool after all. But after they had told their good deeds, they all got into Mrs. Peters's van and rode to the pool.

After they got there, everyone jumped right in at the shallow end.

"Darn, I forgot my swimsuit," said Molly.

Mrs. Peters frowned. It was not like Molly to forget things.

"Well, you can go in the water wearing your shorts," she said.

Molly shook her head. "They're new," she said. "My mom doesn't want me to get them wet. They might fade. I think she's going to dry-clean them."

"How come you forgot your suit?" asked Rachel, pulling a bathing cap over her head and ears to keep her hair dry.

"I was in a hurry," said Molly.

She sat on a bench. She watched the others swim. Some just played in the shallow end. Jody swam across the whole pool. And Kevin dove into the water from the small diving board. Everyone clapped. Roger was busy trying to push Patty's head underwater, but she screamed and gave him a kick.

"Ouch!" said Roger.

"Did you really forget your suit?" asked Mary Beth suspiciously.

Now would be the perfect time for Molly to tell her best friend about her fear of water. Molly hated keeping things from Mary Beth. But when she tried to tell her, something stopped her. It was embarrassing to be a baby about going in the water. But at this rate she would have to sit on a bench at every Pee Wee meeting! Everyone would be suspicious then! She simply had to go in the water sometime.

On the way home Mary Beth said, "Let's go to the pool tomorrow and practice. You missed today so you can make up for it."

"I have to walk Skippy," said Molly.

"You need to practice swimming," Mary Beth said. "You can't get your badge if you can't swim, and you can't swim with no practice."

"I can too," said Molly crossly.

When Kenny and Tim and Tracy asked her to go with them on Thursday, Molly said she couldn't get her hair wet.

On Friday she said she had to go to the mall with her mother.

And on Saturday she said she had a dentist appointment.

"Tuesday is our last practice day at the pool," said Mary Beth on the phone.

It was no use putting it off. Molly had to get wet. On Tuesday she put on her bumblebee suit, took the matching yellow towel her dad had brought home for her, and walked to Mary Beth's house. On the way, she thought Mary Beth was right. She should have practiced swimming. What if she really could swim and didn't know it? Maybe she wasn't as afraid of water as she thought. She was glad she was going to give it a chance. Her dad said always to have a positive attitude. Well, she would. She was on the way to the pool, wasn't she? She'd try the real thing and if it didn't work, she'd have to use plan B.

But when Mary Beth came out of her house, Molly forgot all about her embarrassment. She blurted out, "I can't swim! I'm afraid to put my head under water! How am I going to get my badge?"

Molly felt better already. Someone knew her problem now. Someone who could help her.

"I wish you'd told me before," said Mary Beth thoughtfully. She looked at Molly's bumblebee suit. "My sister could have taught you. And they have swimming lessons at the pool on Mondays. All you need is a little extra help."

"I'll sink and drown," said Molly.

Mary Beth shook her head. "No you won't," she said. "Even little kids like my baby brother don't sink."

Mary Beth was trying to cheer Molly up, but it made her feel worse. The idea that even babies could swim, when she couldn't, was not a cheery thought.

"I'll help you," said Mary Beth. "So will Mrs. Peters."

At the pool, all the Pee Wees were splashing each other and playing water games. The lifeguard sat in his chair with a long pole so that he could reach out and rescue anyone who sank. Molly hoped he wouldn't be reaching out to her.

Jody came up. He liked her bumblebee swimsuit. "It's really cool!" he said.

But Tim put his hands over his eyes as if the suit were blinding him, and some of the boys made buzzing noises and pretended to sting Molly.

"Hey, Duff!" shouted Roger. "Haven't you got a dentist appointment today?" Roger roared as he held his nose and jumped off the side of the pool.

"Don't pay any attention to him," said Mary Beth.

Molly put one foot in the water. That was not too bad. She put the other foot in. Then she walked out till the water was up to her knees. By the time it reached her waist, it felt scary. Pee Wees swam by on all sides of her. Some were floating on their backs. Some were doing the dog paddle. But not one of them looked afraid to get his or her head wet. Molly saw Lisa sitting at the side of the pool, but she was probably just resting.

"Now," said Mary Beth to Molly, "just lie down on the water."

Molly stared at her friend. You could lie down on a bed. Or a couch. Or even the ground. But Molly had never heard of lying down on the water!

"Don't worry," said Mary Beth. "I'll have my arms under you to hold you up." She put her arms out on top of the water.

Arms did not seem safe to Molly. What if she was too heavy? What if someone came by and called to Mary Beth and she forgot she was holding Molly up? What if she forgot she was responsible for Molly's life?

Mary Beth was jiggling her arms. "Come on!" she said.

Molly closed her eyes and lay down. "Don't let me go!" she shouted.

"Kick your feet and paddle your arms!" said Mary Beth.

Molly kicked and paddled. She was moving! But so were Mary Beth's arms!

"We have to go into deeper water," said Mary Beth. "Otherwise you'll touch bottom."

Touching bottom sounded good to Molly. But Mary Beth began walking out farther. Molly kicked and paddled. All of a sudden she felt someone tickling her stomach! Then something pulled her down. Something strong. She felt water in her nose and in her ears and in her mouth. She was sinking and

she couldn't even scream! Was she drowning?

Drowning was definitely too big a price to pay for a badge! *Any* badge! If she somehow lived and did *not* drown, Molly knew one thing for sure. She would move on to plan B, and not try to swim alone again in her whole life!

CHAPTER 6

All Alone Again

When Molly sank to the bottom of the pool, she gave a big push with her feet. She found that it wasn't so deep after all. She stood up, spluttering and coughing. Her ears had water in them, and she couldn't hear too well.

"That darn Roger!" said Mary Beth. "He thinks he's so funny!"

Mary Beth made a face as Roger swam off laughing. Mrs. Peters was waiting for him when he climbed up the ladder. She shook her finger at him and made him sit on a bench while she talked to him.

Then she came over and asked if Molly was all right.

"I guess so," said Molly. "But I don't want to swim anymore."

"Molly is afraid of water," said Mary Beth. "A little."

"Well, Rome wasn't built in a day," said their leader. "This takes time. I think you should get back on the horse and ride."

Molly knew she meant that the pool was a horse, and that Molly should not give up.

This time Mrs. Peters and Mary Beth both held their arms out while Molly kicked and paddled.

"That's good!" said Mrs. Peters. "You just need practice, Molly. Mr. White is coming at two o'clock to give special help to those who need it. I think you'll be his first customer."

Mrs. Peters went off to watch the others,

and Molly wondered if she had heard her correctly. She could not have said that Mr. White, Roger's father, was coming to help her swim! Molly must have misunderstood because of the water in her ears.

"I didn't know Roger's dad was a swimming teacher!" said Mary Beth.

Then it was true. Mary Beth had heard it too.

Just then Mr. White, who looked something like Roger, only bigger, came through the door. Mrs. Peters talked to him awhile, and then pointed to Molly.

This badge was turning into a nightmare! Molly did not want *any* swimming teacher. She especially did not want any relative of Roger White's to help her!

"Hello there," said the man to Molly. "I hear you could use a little help."

His voice was soft and gentle, almost like her own father's. He sat on the edge of the pool and told Molly, and a few others who gathered around, how to relax in the water. "If you relax," he said, "you can't drown."

"Even if his son pulls you under?" whispered Mary Beth into Molly's ear.

Mr. White showed them what he meant. He walked out into the pool and floated on his back just as if he were lying on a lounge chair.

He told Molly how to breathe and how to relax. It sounded easy enough. But when Molly tried, she sank to the bottom again.

"You're too tense," said Mrs. Peters. "You have to loosen up and go with the flow."

If Molly went with the flow, she'd flow right down the drain, she thought.

Rachel came over and helped her. Rat's knees! Did everyone know Molly couldn't swim?

Even Sonny came over and told her one of his secrets for staying afloat.

"I take these huge breaths," he said. "So I

get all full of air, like an inner tube. Then I just float, like this."

Sonny took a couple of noisy gulps of air and floated.

Molly wanted to get out of the water. She was tired of sinking, and her skin was getting all wrinkled like a prune.

As she sat and dangled her legs, Lisa sat down beside her.

"I'm sure glad to find out you can't swim either," she said.

"You can't swim?" shrieked Molly. "Really?"

Lisa nodded. "I'm scared of water. And I thought I was the only one who wouldn't get a badge."

Molly felt better right away. She wouldn't be alone! Instead of just staring at her bumblebee suit, the Pee Wees would stare at Lisa too!

"I keep trying, but I just can't stay up," said Lisa. "No matter what I do."

The girls watched Rachel stand on her head in the water. That didn't matter to Molly now! She had a friend who understood! A friend who could not swim or float or stand on her head! She felt like hugging Lisa.

"I don't mind not getting my badge, if you don't get one too," said Lisa.

"Me too!" shrieked Molly.

Just then Mr. White came over to the girls.

"Let's see if we can turn you into a water sprite," he said to Lisa.

There it was again, that word that was like *elf*!

Lisa did not look happy, but she let Mr. White pull her to her feet and take her into the water.

"I can't swim," she told him. "I keep sinking."

Molly watched them as they stood there. Mr. White was telling her the same things he had told Molly about relaxing. About not being tense. About how she could not sink. Lisa was listening. But Molly knew his advice did not work. She knew it would not help Lisa swim. She wanted to tell Mr. White to just skip it. It was a waste of time.

Mary Beth and Tracy and Kevin came and sat down with Molly.

"I can't believe that guy is Roger's father," said Tracy. "How could a nice guy like him have a son like Roger?"

All the Pee Wees agreed. They shook their heads in wonder.

"Well, it's good his dad likes him," said Mary Beth. "I'll bet his mother took one look at Roger and left home."

That sounded cruel to Molly, but she had to admit it would be hard to love Roger. He was lucky he had a patient dad.

The Pee Wees watched as Mr. White guided Lisa, encouraging her to relax and paddle. Lisa paddled back and forth, back and forth. And then, all of a sudden, Molly

noticed that Mr. White's arms were not holding Lisa up anymore! She was on her own, and she wasn't sinking! She was moving alone on the water! She was *swimming*!

All the Pee Wees burst into applause! They clapped and whistled and shouted. They yelled, "Good for you, Lisa!"

All except Molly. To Molly, Lisa was a traitor. She had lied! Lisa *could* swim. And now Molly had lost her only nonswimming, nonbadge partner, just as fast as she'd found her. Rat's knees, she was back to being the only one without a badge.

CHAPTER 7

Plan B

Lisa came walking out of the pool dripping wet with a big grin on her face. "It's easy!" she said. "It's so easy!"

"That's because my dad is such a good teacher," boasted Roger.

Everyone made a big fuss over Lisa. Mrs. Peters put her arm around her and said, "Well done, Lisa. That's what happens when you hang in there, when you don't give up."

Mrs. Peters looked at Molly when she said that. She seemed to be giving her a message.

"I know you can do it," Lisa said to Molly. "If I can learn, you can learn. Let me show you."

Now Lisa not only was a traitor, she was trying to be a teacher to Molly! Molly hated having everyone feeling sorry for her, even someone who hadn't been able to swim herself ten minutes ago!

"Now just relax," said Lisa. "It's true, it really works."

But Molly was not relaxed. She was mad. She wanted to get out of that pool and go home where she could take her bumblebees off and throw them in a corner.

"Thanks anyway," she muttered to Lisa.

"Well, at least you got wet this time," Sonny said to Molly when they went to the dressing rooms.

That sounded nasty to Molly, but maybe Sonny meant it to be encouraging.

As everyone got dressed and ready to leave, Molly remembered something. Plan B. All was not lost. She would have to think of an artificial way of staying on top of the water.

On the way home, the Pee Wees were kind to Molly. Patty put her arm around her and said, "Next week you'll do it."

Sonny said, "Remember those deep breaths so you get air in you."

And Jody said she could practice in his pool, as soon as it was open.

But that would be too late. Too late for her badge.

When they got to Mary Beth's house, she and Molly sat on the front steps.

"I can't do it," said Molly. "That's all there is to it. I need something to hold me up." She told Mary Beth about Plan B.

"What could we find to hold you up?" asked Mary Beth. "If you wore a safety vest, everyone would see it. It has to be something invisible."

The girls thought and thought.

"Sonny says you need to be full of air to float," said Molly. "I guess I have to swallow an inner tube!"

Mary Beth laughed and waddled along as if she had an inner tube inside her.

"Wait a minute!" she said. "I know something smaller that holds air! Balloons! Balloons float!"

"I can't swallow a balloon!" said Molly.

"You don't swallow it, silly," said Mary Beth. "You put it inside your suit!"

"A balloon won't hold me up," said Molly.

"No, but lots of balloons will," said her friend.

Mary Beth examined Molly's bumblebee swimsuit. "See, it's elastic," she said. "It stretches! We could tuck lots of balloons under it! No one would see them, and they'd keep you afloat! All you'd have to do is kick your legs and arms!"

"Really?" said Molly. It made sense. And it seemed easy.

"Let's go to the toystore and get some," said Mary Beth, jumping up.

Molly ran home and got some of her allowance out of her bank. Then she and Mary Beth got out their bikes and rode to the toystore.

The store had balloons of all colors. The girls picked out ten bright yellow ones.

"In case they show, people will just think they're part of your swimsuit," said Mary Beth.

On the way home, she added, "We'll blow them up on Tuesday. That way they won't get flat before we go."

Mary Beth was so smart! Molly was glad to have her for a best friend. It looked as if there was hope after all that she could get her badge with the others. Molly put the balloons under her pillow, so that they would bring her good dreams.

But they didn't do that. Instead, that night, Molly dreamed that on the way to the pool, the balloons got away from them and flew high over the treetops. No matter how she and Mary Beth chased them, they couldn't catch them. And when she woke up in the morning, Molly was all tired out as if she really had been running.

"It was just a dream," she said to herself. "It won't really happen." And it didn't.

On Tuesday Mary Beth came over and they blew up the balloons.

"Not too big," said Mary Beth. "We don't want them to pop."

When they all were blown up, Molly and Mary Beth squeezed them under the bumblebees. The suit held them in place firmly.

"Wow, this was a good idea," said Mary

Beth. "No way will you sink now! Why didn't we think of this before?"

Molly felt lumpy, but good. "Even if Roger tries to pull me under, I won't sink!" she said.

"Even if every single one of the Pee Wees tries to pull you under, you won't sink!" said Mary Beth.

It wasn't easy to walk with all the lumps around her, but it was a small price to pay for a badge!

When Mary Beth saw Molly's waddly walk, she said, "I think we should meet the others at the pool, instead of riding in Mrs. Peters's van."

"Why?" demanded Molly.

Mary Beth frowned. "If we go over bumps, you might pop. Then everyone would ask questions. You know how nosy Roger and Sonny are."

Molly knew. Mary Beth called Mrs. Peters and said they would meet them at the pool.

"She said okay, but to be on time."

"Let's go," said Molly.

She and Mary Beth started off toward the pool. Molly could not walk very fast. And she couldn't see her feet. She tried to keep up with Mary Beth, but it wasn't easy.

"Don't fall now," said Mary Beth. "You'll lose all your air and we'll really be in trouble."

When they finally got to the pool, the Pee Wees were just getting out of the van. Mrs. Peters was busy counting noses and didn't notice Molly's waddly walk.

But the Pee Wees stared.

"Hey!" shouted Roger. "Look at Molly! Hey, what did you feed those bumblebees that made them so fat?"

"Don't you know it's not polite to call someone fat?" said Mary Beth to him crossly.

"How fat do I look?" cried Molly to her friend.

Mary Beth frowned. "Not very," she said. "Anyway, you can't have everything! You want to get your badge, don't you?"

Molly did. None of the other Pee Wees said anything. But they looked as if they wanted to.

Baby Nick was splashing in the shallow water. He began to paddle with his little arms and legs.

"Look! Nick can swim!" shouted Jody. The Pee Wees all gathered around him and clapped.

"Even a baby can swim," said Molly. "And he hasn't got balloons under his suit."

"Babies learn easily," said Mary Beth.

Mrs. Peters raised her hand for attention.

The time had come. It was time for the Pee Wees to sink or swim.

CHAPTER 8

The Test

"Who wants to be first?" asked Mrs. Peters.

All the hands went up. Even Molly's. She didn't want to be first. But she wanted to get it over with.

But Rachel went first, swimming across the pool gracefully with almost no splashing. There was no doubt about it, Rachel seemed to be good at everything she tried.

Jody swam next, then Patty and Kenny. When Tim swam, he sank.

"Ho ho, no badge for Noon!" shouted Roger.

But Mrs. Peters gave Tim another start, and eventually he paddled across the pool on his own with a lot of splashing.

When it was Roger's turn, he shouted, "Watch this!" He jumped into the pool, holding his nose. The Pee Wees watched, but no Roger came to the top of the pool!

Mrs. Peters looked alarmed, and the lifeguard jumped in to rescue him.

"I didn't need help," said Roger after he had been dragged, dripping and sputtering, to the side of the pool. "I was just staying down there on purpose."

"Sure, he wanted to drown on purpose," joked Rachel.

"This pool is too little," Roger said. "I can dive from that high board. This is baby stuff."

"He's the baby," said Mary Beth. "He wants to dive and he can't even swim."

"It's because he's nervous," said Molly. "He swam before. His dad taught him a long time ago."

Roger turned bright red when Mrs. Peters helped him. Finally he made it, but he looked cross.

"Pride goes before a fall," said Tracy. "That's what my mom says. When you want to show off, things happen."

When it was Sonny's turn, he swam across the pool better than Roger.

"I practiced a lot," he said. "At the lake. My mom made me."

"Molly Duff is next," said Mrs. Peters.

Molly waddled toward the water. Mrs. Peters squinted across the pool at her, and looked as if she was going to say something. But before she could, Molly was in the water. She began to paddle, and wonder of wonders, she did not sink! She rode very high on the water, like a canoe! Her face did not even get wet!

But as she paddled, she heard a pop! Then another one! It sounded like when her dad pulled a cork out of a bottle of wine!

Molly paddled on. There was only half the width of the pool to go now, and she'd have her badge.

Pop pop pop! Now Molly's face was getting wet! But Molly paddled on, faster and faster! She gave one last shove, and made it to the ladder on the other side of the pool! She did it! Plan B had worked!

Everyone cheered when Molly got out of the pool.

"Good for you!" said Mrs. Peters.

"What happened to your bumblebees?" shouted Sonny. "They aren't fat anymore!"

Molly looked down at the bumblebees. Everyone must have noticed they had been thin, then fat, then thin again. But Sonny was right. They were not fat anymore! And Molly would walk without waddling.

"The balloons are gone," whispered Molly to Mary Beth.

"They popped," said Mary Beth, nodding. "You swam across most of the pool without them!"

Molly could not believe her ears. Plan B had turned into Plan A. She had actually won her badge legally!

"Hey, Duff," asked Roger suspiciously, "what happened to those fat bees?"

Molly pretended she did not know what Roger meant. All was well that ended well, as Tracy's mom would probably say.

After Mrs. Peters had seen everyone swim, the Pee Wees played water games. Then they sang their Pee Wee song and said their pledge right there at the pool.

When they were ready to leave, Nick toddled out of the water with something in his hand. Something yellow. He held it out to his mother.

"Boon!" he said. "Boon!"

"Why, yes, it is," said his mother. "It's a yellow balloon! I wonder how it got into the pool!"

But Nick was picking up more yellow balloons from the water! They were flat. And they had holes in them. Molly turned bright red.

"Should I tell her they're mine?" Molly asked Mary Beth.

"Why?" said Mary Beth. "My mom says to let sleeping dogs lie. It means let things alone."

And sure enough, Mrs. Peters just took the balloons from Nick and threw them into the trash can. There was no use looking for trouble, thought Molly. Mary Beth's mother was probably right.

CHAPTER 9

A Badge at Last

When Molly got home she decided she should tell her parents about plan B. It didn't seem honest to keep things from them. She didn't like to keep secrets from her own family. Besides, she felt as if she would explode if she didn't confess to someone besides Mary Beth.

Her parents listened while Molly told them about how she had sunk at first, and how the balloons had held her up.

"But when they popped, it didn't matter. I swam by myself without sinking!" she said.

"Well, I think you learned something, Molly," her father said. "It would have been much easier if you had come and told us the problem and learned to swim the right way."

"You worked so hard to pretend," said her mother. "And in the end you swam alone anyway! You could have done it without all that fuss."

What her parents said made sense. But Molly never seemed to do things the easy way. She was stuck with a wild imagination. She was stuck doing things the hard way. But she had to admit, maybe she had just imagined that she couldn't swim!

Anyway, it felt good to confess. Now only the good things were left, like getting the badges and seeing Jody's new pool. And soon the phone rang and Mrs. Peters said that they would do both of those together.

"We are going to give out the badges at Jody's swimming party tomorrow at two o'clock," she said.

The next day the Pee Wees couldn't wait. Molly watched the clock and counted off the minutes as they went by. At last, at ten minutes to two, Mary Beth came to her door. Molly picked up her beach bag, and the two friends ran all the way to Jody's.

When they got there, they saw a sign on the lawn that said WELCOME TO THE PEE WEE POOL PARTY!

Behind the sign was Jody's house. It seemed to Molly to reach to the sky. The yard was full of flowers, and there was a big tent set up with tables full of food inside. Music floated out from the house, and balloons and paper lanterns hung from the trees.

"I don't want to look at any more balloons," muttered Molly.

"Wow!" said Mary Beth. "Jody *is* rich!"

The girls had known that Jody had a nice
house, but they had not been inside it before.

"Do we go to the front door, or to the
tent?" Mary Beth asked Molly.

"I think it's polite to go to the door," said
Molly.

The girls walked up the smooth winding
ramp for Jody's wheelchair. The doorbell
played a song when the girls pushed it.

A woman with a white apron on opened
the door and said, "Come right in!" Molly
knew it wasn't Jody's mother. It must be a
maid!

"You can join the others out at the pool,"
the woman said. "They're all waiting for
you."

The girls walked slowly through the big
house, sinking into the fat rugs and looking

up at the big crystal lights. At the back of the house was a long porch with comfortable chairs, and when they went out the door, Molly could not believe her eyes.

The big blue pool stretched before them in the sun. There were trees, bushes, and colorful flowers growing around it in all the right places. There were pool chairs and tables, and beach balls and rafts and inner tubes. A man greeted the girls and offered them cold drinks.

When Jody spotted them, he left everyone else and wheeled his chair in their direction.

"It's our first pool party!" he said with a big smile.

"It's great," said Mary Beth.

Molly saw Mrs. Peters stretched out on a lounge chair, with little Nick. Roger was chasing Sonny around and around a little fountain in the garden. Kevin was diving into the pool. And Lisa and Patty and

Kenny were in the dining tent putting shrimp with red sauce on flowery paper plates.

When he saw all the food, Roger came running up shouting and whistling.

Sonny's mother tried to keep Roger from putting too much food on his plate. She was there, thought Molly, because she was the Pee Wees' assistant leader. In a little while Mr. White came in too. Probably because he'd helped them learn to swim and get their badges, Molly decided.

"This tile around the pool is from Italy," said Jody, pointing.

If someone else had said that, it would have sounded like bragging, thought Molly. But it never did when Jody said it. You could tell he was proud of his family's home.

"This is like the movies," said Mary Beth, holding a drink with pink ice and a tiny umbrella stuck into a piece of orange.

The girls sat down in the pool chairs to drink their drinks. There were wonderful yard smells in the air, of good food, sweet flowers, and chlorine from the pool.

As they sat there, Jody's mom and dad came around to welcome each Pee Wee. Then Mr. George gave a little talk, telling them how glad he was to have them at the party, and to have a good time and enjoy swimming.

After that Mrs. Peters got up and made a few announcements. Most of the Pee Wees were too excited to listen. She thanked the Georges for having them all there, and then she said, "We'll all have some wonderful food now, and while we are waiting an hour to go in the water, we'll hand out the badges."

As Roger and Sonny dove into the buffet table again, eating and talking at the same time, Ashley said, "Mrs. Peters, I know what our next badge should be. It should be a badge for good manners." Ashley glared at the boys.

"Those boys act like cavemen," said Rachel. "They push and shove at the table and talk with their mouths full."

Mrs. Peters laughed and said that a manners badge was not a bad idea.

As they were eating, Mrs. Peters called out their names, and each one of the Pee Wees came up and got his or her brand-new badge. It was a badge that Molly would never forget earning. Rat's knees, it was beautiful!

As soon as the hour was up, the Pee Wees scrambled into Jody's new pool. They played water games, and Mr. George led them in a water race.

Then Jody and Kevin showed Molly how to do the jellyfish float.

"When you go underwater, you don't have to worry. You'll come right to the top," said Jody.

Molly had her badge. She didn't have to learn anything else new. But she could see that Jody wanted her to learn. And besides, it was fun being in the pool now that she didn't *have* to be!

Jody's pool must have had some magic potion in it, because Molly did come right to the top! Instead of sinking, she popped up like a jack-in-the-box!

"The main thing is not to panic," said Kevin. "You have to relax."

Molly knew that, but it had never worked before. This time she trusted her friends. Jody and Kevin would not let her down. They would not trick her the way Roger would.

Now she could swim, and she could float. Without balloons in her suit.

Rat's knees! It looked as if it was going to be a fun-filled summer in Jody's new pool, with the Pee Wees!

Pee Wee Scout Song
(to the tune of "Old MacDonald Had a Farm")

Scouts are helpers, Scouts have fun
Pee Wee, Pee Wee Scouts!
We sing and play when work is done,
Pee Wee, Pee Wee Scouts!

With a good deed here,
And an errand there,
Here a hand, there a hand,
Everywhere a good hand.

Scouts are helpers, Scouts have fun,
Pee Wee, Pee Wee Scouts!

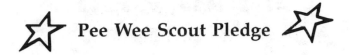
Pee Wee Scout Pledge

We love our country
And our home,
Our school and neighbors too.

As Pee Wee Scouts
We pledge our best
In everything we do.